N E LINCS LIBRARIES
5 4073 01008506 8

How to Hide a Lion

KT-421-424

NORTH EAST LINCOLNSHIRE
LIBRARIES
WITHDRAWN
FROM STOCK
AUTHORISED: Helen Stephens

NORTH EAST LINCOLNSHIRE COUNCIL	
01008506	
Bertrams	20/08/2012
	£6.99

ALISON GREEN BOOKS

One hot day,
a lion strolled
into a market square
to buy a hat.

But the townspeople were scared of lions,

so he ran away.

He ran as fast and as far as he could . . .

. . . and hid in a house in a garden. It was a play house,
and it belonged to a small girl called Iris.
"You can't hide there," said Iris, who wasn't scared of lions.
"That house is too small for you."

They went inside, so Iris could hide the lion properly. They had to be quiet, as mums and dads can be funny about having a lion in the house.

The lion let Iris pull the
leaves out of his mane . . .

. . . and he showed her his
paw where he had stepped
on something sharp.
"I'll put a plaster on that," said Iris.

It wasn't easy hiding a lion.

He was just too big . . .

too fluffy . . .

and too heavy, especially
when he was asleep.
And lions sleep a lot.

But when no one was looking,
the lion could come out to play.

They just had to be careful
not to be too noisy.

One evening, Iris's dad said, "They still haven't found that lion."
"I bet he's a kind lion," said Iris, from behind the sofa.
"There's no such thing as a kind lion," said her mum. "All lions will eat you."

The lion was worried,
but Iris comforted him.

Then she read him his favourite story. It was about a tiger who came to tea. He fell asleep halfway through, because lions sleep a lot.

And that was how everything went wrong.

Iris heard her mum coming up the stairs,

but it's hard to wake
a sleeping lion.

However, most lions will wake up
if a mum screams at them.

AARGH!

The lion raced out of the house . . .

The
Angel
Inn

. . . and found a hiding place where he could
still see Iris whenever she came into town.

Nobody noticed him.

Not the townspeople. Not even Iris.

And certainly not the two burglars, who broke into the Town Hall and stole every single one of the Lord Mayor's candlesticks.

But the lion noticed them.

With a huge
ROAR!
he leapt off his pedestal . . .

. . . and stood on both the burglars
till the police came.

All the townspeople were amazed – except for Iris, who said, "I told you he was a kind lion."

And that surprised everyone.

Now the lion was a hero. He didn't have to hide any more.
The townspeople held a special parade for him.
The Mayor said he could have anything he wanted.

The lion thought for a moment.
Then he asked for . . .

. . . a hat!

Which was all he'd come to town for in the first place.

"It really suits you," said Iris.

To the Martins

First published in the UK in 2012 by
Alison Green Books
An imprint of Scholastic Children's Books
Euston House, 24 Eversholt Street
London NW1 1DB, UK
A division of Scholastic Ltd
www.scholastic.co.uk
London – New York – Toronto – Sydney – Auckland
Mexico City – New Delhi – Hong Kong

Copyright © 2012 Helen Stephens

HB ISBN: 978 1 407120 66 9
PB ISBN: 978 1 407121 61 1

All rights reserved.
Printed in Singapore.

10 9 8 7 6 5 4 3 2 1

The moral rights of Helen Stephens have been asserted.

Papers used by Scholastic Children's Books are made
from wood grown in sustainable forests.